# Squares Anthology

by

Noel Lorenz

Maelys

A Maelys Presentation

A Maelys Presentation

# Dedicated to

*The Mintakans*

A Maelys Presentation

# Contents

# Preface

Squares Anthology is an initiative by Noel Lorenz to spread awareness about the sweetness of short stories of 22 words, 44 words, and 66 words. These are categorized in their respective segments called squares.

The presentation of a poem is of utmost importance. During Covid19, many people have taken up poetry. All we found were stories written in long poetry format. Most were not even poems. The reason was they just kept writing without a structure in mind. To alleviate that symptom, Noel Lorenz came up with the idea of the Squares Anthology. It provided writers with three squares to choose from before they started writing. This would make them think. Hopefully, this gave the writers a good push to organize their thoughts.

The idea was to help people and budding writers to get their thoughts together and present it precisely.

This is just a start and we are hoping that we can do more square anthologies in the coming time.

-   Noel Lorenz

15 April 2023, Kolkata, India

# About the Book

Squares Anthology is an initiative by Noel Lorenz to spread awareness about the sweetness of short stories of 22 words, 44 words, and 66 words. These are categorized in their respective segments called squares.

In this book, we have international writers trying their hands at short stories of 22 words, 44 words, and 66 words each.

Hope you find this book beautiful as you yourself are.

**The author**

# Acknowledgements

To the Participants for taking their precious time to stick to the rules and trying their best to make this book a success.

A Maelys Presentation

# 1st Square

(22 words stories)

A Maelys Presentation

# Noel Lorenz

A Maelys Presentation

## BIO

**Noel Lorenz** is a novelist and a poet from the City of Joy, India. He has been successfully writing haiku for over 3 years. He has a love for literature and a mind that tries to think out of the box. He has invented a few types of poetry that have been loved and written internationally — Noelo Poems and Hug Poetry are two of such inventions. His horror/mystery debut novel is now available.

## The Wait

Life was good until he came back from exile and was framed for a murder. He's being tried at the Supreme Court.

A Maelys Presentation

# Maid Corbic

A Maelys Presentation

## BIO

Maid Corbic from Tuzla, 22 years old. In his spare time he writes poetry that repeatedly praised as well as rewarded. He also selflessly helps others around him, and he is moderator of the World Literature Forum WLFPH.

A Maelys Presentation

## Birds Eat Humans

Birds ate people, taking meat from their heads. That's the tastiest part for us. And we are afraid. There is no Sun.

A Maelys Presentation

# Seema Bhatnagar

A Maelys Presentation

## BIO

Seema Bhatnagar, a lawyer, writer and a poet at heart. She is an alumnus of Canning College, where she obtained her Masters Degree and two Bachelor's degree one in Sociology and Economics and the other in Law. Regular contributor at many writing websites and as Co Author for Anthologies.

# यादें

याद की एक खिड़की खुली क्या रह गई कि यादों ने मौका मिलते ही पूरे वज़ूद को अपने आग़ोश में ले लिया।

# Jacek Wilkos

A Maelys Presentation

# BIO

Jacek Wilkos is an engineer from Poland. He is addicted to buying books, he loves black coffee, dark ambient music and riding his bike. His stories were published in numerous anthologies by many publications.

## The Thin White Line

A thin white line was a border between two lives - the grey he lived and the colorful he was regularly escaping to.

A Maelys Presentation

# Edward Ahern

A Maelys Presentation

## BIO

Ed Ahern resumed writing after forty odd years in foreign intelligence and international sales. He's had over three hundred stories and poems published so far, and six books. Ed works the other side of writing at Bewildering Stories, where he manages a posse of nine review editors.

## The Caregiver

"Here's your coffee and reading pillow, breakfast coming shortly." "I'm sorry you're feeling pukey." "It's just payback for years of tolerating me."

# Anwesa Maity

A Maelys Presentation

# BIO

Anwesa is a 19 year old writer from the peaceful town of Siliguri hoping to make her way into people's hearts through her poetry, short write-ups and quotes. She has been a part of several anthologies and looks forward to be published as a solo author in the future.

## Two Fathers

As the night grew, both the fathers tenderly tucked in their kids to sleep. One with a blanket, the other with rags.

# Kalamkaar

A Maelys Presentation

BIO

इनका नाम कलमकार है ये उत्तराखंड के रहनेवाले है, मगर मेरठ मे रह रहे हैइन्होने सह   !इनको लिखना और पढ़ना पसंद है ! लेखक के रूप मे2100+ अन्थोलॉजी मे काम किया है और 1800+ प्रमाण पत्र जीते है! इन्होने 28 फेब्रुअरी 2020 से लिखना शुरू किया था!

## धोखा

धोखा देकर वफ़ा की बात करती होरकीब से नज़दीकिया बढ़या  !
वादे जन्म के करती हो !रुस्वा करके उल्फत को !करती हो!

# Athira A.

A Maelys Presentation

# BIO

Athira A. is a young poetess from Ernakulam, Kerala. She has been writing for 15 years as her passion. Athira has compiled many anthologies. Book reading and reviewing are also her major hobbies.

## A Lone Soul

She was not at all surprised on hearing his decision to sunder. After all, she was the only one who craved love!

A Maelys Presentation

# 2nd Square

(44 words stories)

A Maelys Presentation

# Uplaksh Singh Bedi

A Maelys Presentation

## BIO

Ink flows in his vein, Words flow in his arteries, as they reach to heart they become one of his poems. Poetry is his soul and gardening is his body. Uplaksh Singh Bedi, a 17 year old who is the author of a solo book and has also been a co-author in many anthologies. Instagram id:- @_blooming_ink_

## Loneliness

Nothing to do. No one to speak. Feeling stressed. Thinking deep. Drowning in the sea of emotions. Seeing here and there. Knowing I am alone. Everyone left. Noone remained. Heart full of cry. Pleading for support. Begging for kindness. But no one is there.

# Divyanshi Singhal

A Maelys Presentation

## BIO

Divyanshi Singhal in aspiring writer with keen interest in poetry.

## Can We Meet Again

It was heavily raining. I bumped into a stranger at the edge of a street. Her brown hair, that red scarf, and that heavenly scent of plumeria, holding a blue umbrella. All that she had said, "You can take it, you need it more."

A Maelys Presentation

# Nikita Munshi Aggarwal

A Maelys Presentation

## BIO

Nikita is a Mumbai based poet and writer. She launched her debut poetry book in 2021. Previously, she has worked as a management consultant, spending 5 years in the strategy and risk space. Nikita has an appetite for the extraordinary and has traveled to 22 countries.

## Little Joys

It reached me at noon. I saw the package, opened it and stared for a few minutes, misty eyed. My heart started beating faster and my palms got sweaty. I flipped it over and saw the picture, and in that moment I was happy.

A Maelys Presentation

# Adesiyan Oluwapelumi

A Maelys Presentation

## BIO

Adesiyan Oluwapelumi, TPC XI, is a genre-bending creative writer who scribes from Ibadan, Nigeria. He won an Honourable Mention in the 2022 Coexist Lit International Metamorphosis Writing Contest.

**Vignette of a boy in a world of little compassion.**


Dejected, the little boy trots to the back of the ice cream truck and bows his head into the burrows of his arms like chitons in a stream of boulders,tears drizzling down his cheeks. A little girl comes and offers him her cone.


A Maelys Presentation

# Natalya Patolot

A Maelys Presentation

## BIO

Natalya Patolot is a Communication Technology Management student at the Ateneo de Manila University. She is also the Co-Founder and CEO of The Indiependent Collective, a media startup that aims to empower the Filipino youth and push boundaries through socially-engaged conversations.

## Virus

She takes pictures as he smiles. She rants as he listens. She undresses as he watches. He had information to this woman's life at his fingertips. A simple tap on his phone was all he needed to see her, yet she doesn't know him.

# W. J. Manares

A Maelys Presentation

## BIO

W. J. Manares a. k. a. Willer Jun Araneta Manares is a one-of-a-kind persona in the literary scene of Aklan - the oldest province in the Philippines. He usually writes Science Fiction and Fantasy. A NLHFian by heart.

## Fusion of Confusion

Sometimes, my heart tells me to stop loving. But my mind keeps on thinking about the advantages that love can bring in my entire life. So, I allowed them to discuss this matter together. And they're still arguing right now. What a confusing situation!

# 3rd Square

## (66 words stories)

# Sheikh Fajar

A Maelys Presentation

## BIO

Sheikh Fajar is an eminent writer from Kashmir who pens down poems mostly about life, love, compassion, kindness and nature of human hearts.She has co-authored many books and is author of an e-book. For her writings, she has also been selected for IBR 2022.

## The Strange Bond

When you get hardships, my heart also aches .When you suffer in life, I also feel pain. Perhaps I don't care but there's just an unusual bond between us. I'm so busy in your love - without hearing your voice, I can't sleep. Without seeing your face, feeling your essence, I don't get peace. Perhaps, I don't care for you, there's just an unusual bond between us.

A Maelys Presentation

# Rie Sheridan Rose

A Maelys Presentation

## BIO

Rie Sheridan Rose's prose appears in numerous anthologies. In addition, she has authored twelve novels, six poetry chapbooks, and dozens of song lyrics. She tweets as @RieSheridanRose.

## The River Soothes

She stared into the water, mind racing in a thousand directions. The river was deep and cold here under the bridge. The bridge supposed to link the halves of the town, but instead accentuating the divide. He'd left her. Said they were too different. Refused to discuss their mutual problem... She lifted her chin, let go and stepped forward. The cold water washed away all sins.

# Kelli J Gavin

A Maelys Presentation

## BIO

Kelli J Gavin of Carver, Minnesota is a Writer and Professional Organizer. 400+ pieces in over 50 publications. Two books were released in 2019. www.kellijgavin.blogspot.com

## I Miss Them

I have idolized the man my big brother had become after dad died. Marcus left three weeks ago, I guess I am in charge now even though I am only eleven. Chopping wood for the fire and catching fish for dinner are at the top of my list for today. I miss my dad and I miss Marcus. I miss mom even though she's still here.

A Maelys Presentation

# Binod Dawadi

A Maelys Presentation

## BIO

My name is Binod Dawadi from Purano Naikap 13, Kathmandu, Nepal. My date of birth is 2053 - 12 – 2. I have completed my Masters Degree from TU with Major in English. I like to read and write literary forms. My hobbies are dancing, singing, reading and writing. I have written many poems, stories, and other forms of literature.

## Sun And Water

There were two friends Sun and Water. One day they decided to change law. Then Sun tell Water let's change. Then Water told Sun come on you today stay at land and I will stay at sky. Then Sun obeys and do they do that. After that all living beings died because of heat of the Sun. Water cannot find it's space to flow in sky.

A Maelys Presentation

# Til Kumari Sharma

A Maelys Presentation

## BIO

Ms. Til Kumari Sharma was born in Bhorle- Hile, Paiyun 7, Parbat, West Nepal. She is known as Pushpa too. Her parents are Mr. Hari Prasad Bashyal/ Basel Sharma ( Mayor of Village Assembly in the time of Kingdom ) and Mrs. Liladevi Bhusal Bashyal/ Basel.

## Love of Misuse

Once, heroine of earth "Pushpa" was deceived in love. Her real love was misused by lover after her engagement. The boy was Sudan Sangaula. The girl was Pushpa Neupane. She was fired in gate of boy's home. He was looking her firing body. The lust of boy did not secure her eternal love. Beautiful lady in Kathmandu Nepal was in death after separation of love engagement.

# W. J. Manares

A Maelys Presentation

# BIO

W. J. Manares a. k. a. Willer Jun Araneta Manares is a one-of-a-kind persona in the literary scene of Aklan - the oldest province in the Philippines. He usually writes Science Fiction and Fantasy. A NLHFian by heart.

## Pareidolia

As Juan walked his way to the nearest store, he stared above himself and saw an unusual cloud. He was amazed so he took a photograph before the formation had disappeared. He was a fan of a phenomenon called Pareidolia, a self-perception of images that actually don't exist. As he observed the cloudy sky a little longer, he suddenly remembered that his camera has no film.

# Sukanya Biswal

A Maelys Presentation

## BIO

She is Graduate in BSc in Zoology from the College of IGNOU, New Delhi. She is Graduate in Adv Post Graduation Diploma in Computer Application from the college Bachelor of Computer Education (I.T.).

## Creation of the world

Lord Mpungu, the greatest god created the earth and the sky, created two human beings – a man and a woman; to whom the mind was given. But till now he had not given his heart to these two men. Lord Mpungu had four children. Moon, Sun, Darkness and Rain. He called all four together and had said, "I want to retire now. And send a heart."

# About the Author

**Noel Lorenz** is a novelist and a poet from the City of Joy, India. He has been successfully writing haiku for over 3 years. He has a love for literature and a mind that tries to think out of the box. He has invented a few types of poetry that have been loved and written internationally — Noelo Poems and Hug Poetry are two of such inventions. His horror/mystery debut novel is now available.

Noel Lorenz is the founder of Noel Lorenz House of Fiction (NLHF), a publishing house based in Kolkata and operating globally. NLHF has strived to bring the unheard authors from India and Africa to the global platform. He was also awarded the Gandhi Mandela International Award for uplifting African Literature.

He was also awarded the Miguel de Cervantes Literary Award for his contributions to world literature.

Currently, he is writing haiku daily and looking forward to working with his new story ideas.

www.noellorenz.com

A Maelys Presentation

A Maelys Presentation

www.ingramcontent.com/pod-product-compliance
Lightning Source LLC
Chambersburg PA
CBHW071233130726

47998CB00003B/926